DANNY, DENNY, AND THE DANCING DRAGON

Once Upon a Dance

ILLUSTRATED BY ANKA WILLEMS

Dedicated to Cara, Erin, and Cassandra, for making everything better.

Danny, Denny, and the Dancing Dragon
A Dance-It-Out Creative Movement Story for Young Movers

© 2021 Once Upon a Dance   Redmond, WA

Illustrated by Anka Willems, www.ankawillems.nl

Layout in collaboration with Adrian Hoffman

All 2021 book sales donated to ballet companies struggling under COVID-19

Each Dance-It-Out story is a kids' dance performance ready for the imagination stage.
In this volume, Danny can't wait to teach his new little brother to dance. He's disappointed when
the baby doesn't have any moves. But Danny's baby brother has an amazing surprise in store for him.
Ballerina Konora helps readers express movement alongside Danny, Denny, and Kadessa the Dragon.

LCCN: 2021925517

ISBN 978-1-7368-7507-0 (paperback); 978-1-7368-7508-7 (ebook); 978-1-7368-7509-4 (hardcover)

Juvenile Fiction: Imagination & Play (Juvenile Fiction: Animals: Dragons; Juvenile Fiction: Performing Arts: Dance)

First Edition

Other Once Upon a Dance Titles:
Joey Finds His Jump!: A Dance-It-Out Creative Movement Story for Young Movers
Petunia Perks Up: A Dance-It-Out Movement and Meditation Story
Princess Naomi Helps a Unicorn: A Dance-It-Out Creative Movement Story for Young Movers
The Cat with the Crooked Tail: A Dance-It-Out Creative Movement Story for Young Movers
Brielle's BIrthday Ball: A Dance-It-Out Creative Movement Story for Young Movers
Mira Monkey's Magic Mirror Adventure: A Dance-It-Out Creative Movement Story for Young Movers
Belluna's Big Adventure in the Sky: A Dance-It-Out Creative Movement Story for Young Movers
Dancing Shapes: Ballet and Body Awareness for Young Dancers
More Dancing Shapes: Ballet and Body Awareness for Young Dancers
Nutcracker Dancing Shapes: Shapes and Stories from Konora's Twenty-Five Nutcracker Roles
Dancing Shapes with Attitude: Ballet and Body Awareness for Young Dancers
Konora's Shapes: Poses from Dancing Shapes for Creative Movement & Ballet Teachers
More Konora's Shapes: Poses from More Dancing Shapes for Creative Movement & Ballet Teachers
Ballerina Dreams Ballet Inspiration Journal/Notebook

Hello Fellow Dancer,

My name is Ballerina Konora. I love stories, adventures, and ballet, and I'm glad you're here today!

Will you be my dance partner and act out the story along with me and Danny?

I've included descriptions of movements that express the story. You can decide whether to use these ideas or create your own moves. Be safe, of course, and do what works for you in your space. If you want to settle in and enjoy the pictures first, that's fine.

Konora

P.S. You don't have to be a dragon to act like Kadessa. And, boy or girl, you can act out all the characters in this story.

ONCE UPON A DANCE, Danny returned from school to exciting news. His little brother, Denny, had finally arrived. Danny couldn't wait to play with his new brother. He'd been looking forward to meeting him for so long. He was especially excited about teaching him to dance. Dancing was one of Danny's favorite things in the whole wide world.

Danny tried to teach his brother how to do a *plié*, but it didn't work. It turns out babies can't even stand! Why hadn't someone explained this to Danny?!

Let's pretend we're Danny demonstrating some pliés.
Bend your knees while keeping the rest of your body still and your back tall.

Then relax on the floor as if you're a new baby who can hardly even move your head. Your muscles are mostly turned off.

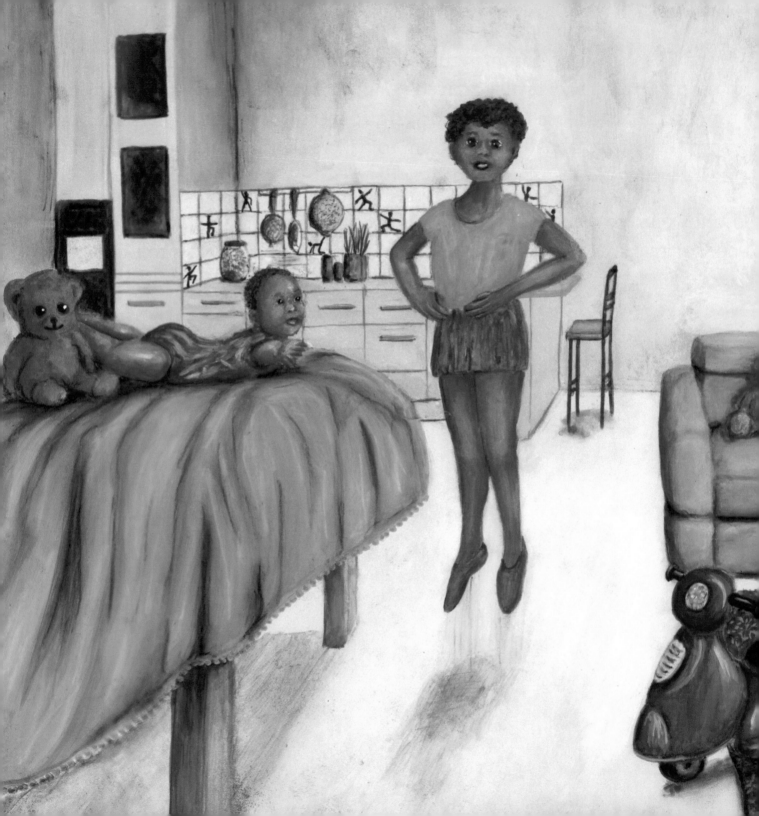

Even though Denny was a useless blob as far as dance partners go, Danny had to admit he was a cute little blob. As the weeks and months passed, Danny grew to love his little brother, and he discovered ways to play with him.

One day, as Danny was practicing his *chassés*, he noticed the baby happily rocking on all fours like he wanted to dance.

It looked like so much fun that Danny decided to get on his hands and knees, too. Danny followed the baby's lead as he rolled onto his back. When Denny kicked up his feet in the air and let out a joyful, "Goo-goo, ga-ga!" a most remarkable thing happened!

To chassé like Danny, gallop and giddy-up. Keep one foot in front the whole time. Take a step forward and then gather both legs up underneath you in a mini-jump.

Then we'll dance like Denny and rock back and forth on our hands and knees. Before you roll over, make sure there's nothing in your way. I always check for my cats—they love to visit me whenever I stretch or dance on the floor. Once we're upside down, we could even let out a happy *goo-goo, ga-ga*!

A dragon appeared. Danny couldn't believe his eyes! The dragon hovered above his brother, as if perched on Denny's hands and feet. It was as if Denny had summoned the dragon with his baby-talk!

With his mouth hanging open, Danny watched as the dragon mirrored Denny's movements as though they were dancing together.

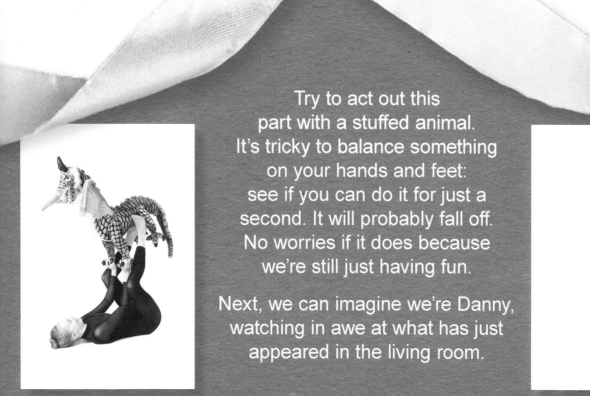

Try to act out this part with a stuffed animal. It's tricky to balance something on your hands and feet: see if you can do it for just a second. It will probably fall off. No worries if it does because we're still just having fun.

Next, we can imagine we're Danny, watching in awe at what has just appeared in the living room.

Danny was still in shock to see a dragon in his house, but he was also stunned that his brother wasn't surprised. In fact, the baby was rolling around with the dragon as if he'd done this before.

Denny looked over at Danny and said, "Goo-goo, ga-ga!"

I think he's inviting me to join their dance, thought Danny. He was nervous as the dragon hopped off Denny and walked on all fours toward him. But as the dragon stood up on her hind legs and did a little twirl, Danny got excited. Here was a dance partner who could do ballet with him!

Back on the floor
for a little baby-dragon dance.
Don't forget your *goo-goo, ga-gas*.

Then let's be the dragon.
We are powerful animals
walking with our feet and
hands touching the ground.
Then stand up and spin around.

Together they did jumps and kicks and twirls. All the while, Denny babbled happily as if he was making the music for their dance.

The dragon paused to take a deep, long breath; then she let out a sigh. When she sighed, a little bit of smoke came out of her nostrils! "Hello, my name is Kadessa," said the dragon.

"I'm Danny. And I see you've met my baby brother, Denny."

His brother added a little "Goo-goo, ga-ga!"

Let's be like the dancing duo and do a few jumps. We'll start by bending our knees, then try to jump ourselves into the air by pushing our feet down. Then let's send each leg out to the front in a kick. And we'll do another twirl or two, picking up our feet to turn ourselves around.

Then it's time for a nice deep breath. Normally, I'd sigh though my mouth, but let's try one like Kadessa's and let the air escape through our noses.

"Where did you learn to dance so well?" asked Danny.

"Oh, I've danced all over the world! Would you like to see some of my travels?" Kadessa took in another deep breath and breathed out a stream of fire! Danny watched in awe as the fire started moving around to form images of some of the incredible sights Kadessa had seen: castles, pirate ships, and a forest of unicorns.

Wouldn't it
be fun to re-create
the things Kadessa shows us?
Hmm, how can we make a castle?
I think we should use our strong muscles
to form whatever shape we choose.

I'm going to pretend my whole
body is the pirate ship, but you
could also create a ship shape with
just your hands, arms, or legs.

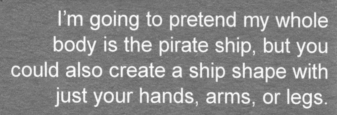

How will you make the shape of a unicorn in the forest?
I'm making a horn with my hands, but there are all kinds
of ways to pretend to be a unicorn.

Mesmerized by the dragon's pictures, Denny reached out to touch the fiery images. Quickly, Danny reached to stop him. Upset at being held back, the baby let out a shriek—and with that, Kadessa disappeared.

Almost as if
we are Denny in a trance,
let's stretch our arm out and
imagine delicately touching the
smoke. There's a very slow, careful
quality to this simple move.

Afterward, Danny wondered if meeting Kadessa had been a dream. Could it really have happened that a dragon was here in his house?

But then, one day, it happened again. Danny's brother rolled on his back with his feet it in the air and said, "Goo-goo, ga-ga!" And again, there was Kadessa, right in their living room.

Back to our favorite *goo-goo, ga-ga* pose. Upside down we go. It sure is good exercise getting in and out of this position.

Danny loved Kadessa's visits. He never knew when the next visit would be, but he always looked forward to their dancing duets and watching her fiery magic. She'd recently shown them queens, trolls and fairies!

Let's
be the fanciful creatures
from Kadessa's pictures. With our imaginary
crowns, we feel like powerful queens and kings!
Ready, set… let's be mean, nasty, stomping trolls.
The fairy is almost the opposite. Ready, set… delicate fairies.
I feel dainty and graceful.

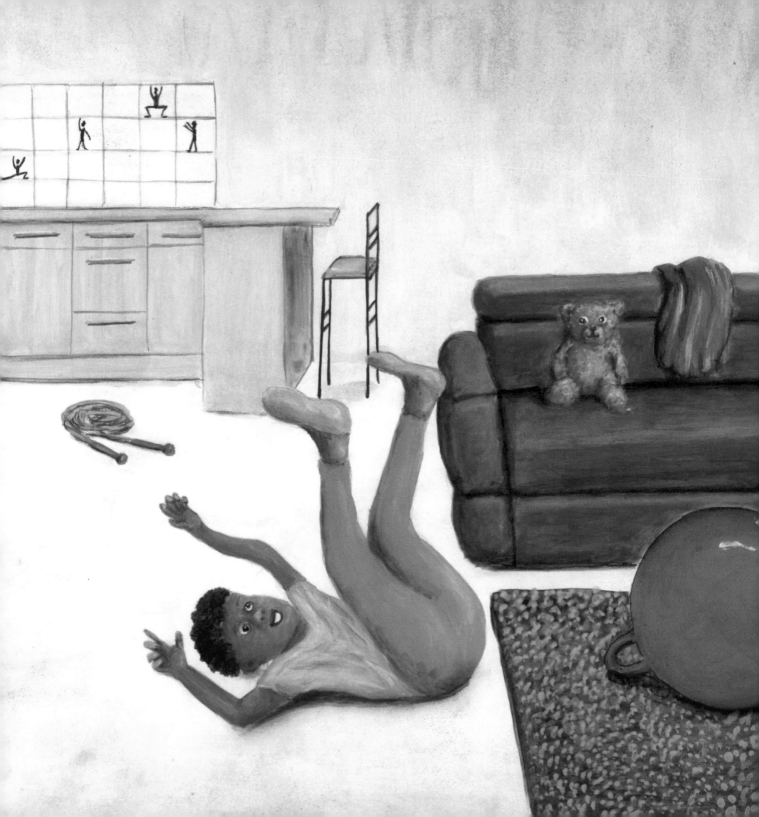

One day, when the baby was napping, Danny yearned to have another dance with Kadessa. But how could he make her appear? He remembered his brother's baby-talk and wondered if they really were magic words. He whispered, "Goo-goo, ga-ga!" But nothing happened. Then he remembered the baby's favorite position. He checked to make sure no one was watching, got on his back, kicked his feet in the air, and said, "Goo-goo, ga-ga!"

Shall we whisper a small *goo-goo, ga-ga?*

Then here we go again to our upside-down pose, feet up, and a stronger *goo-goo, ga-ga.*

Kadessa appeared, just for Danny! He was so happy to see her again, he got up and started jumping happy jumps. Kadessa showed Danny new dances from far-off lands, and they danced and laughed together.

Let's jump up and down with delight. I like to tap my fingertips together, but you can show your happiness in whatever way you feel. We can even make ourselves smile. I feel kind of funny, but you know what? Smiling is good for you.

Do you want to try the tricky move in the picture? Put one foot on the ground, and the other leg out to the side. Then, as if you were making the biggest-possible circle with your toe paintbrush, bring your circling leg forward until you bump into your other leg. Quickly lift the inside leg and step over the circling leg. Keep sending the circling leg around and around.

Now that Danny knew how to summon Kadessa, he would call her every so often. But he tried to mostly summon her when Denny was awake, because the baby was a great audience. And soon, his baby brother would be able to toddle alongside them and perform some new dance moves as well!

Do you think it's more fun to dance with an audience? Most of us like it, but some people would rather dance alone.

Maybe you could make up a little dragon duet for your audience. Put your real or imaginary stuffed animal on your legs and try to spin it around using your feet and hands. Straighten your legs and arms as far as they can go and let your dragon soar into the air.

Danny learned that sometimes, there's magic found in simple, childlike things. Who knew that a little bit of baby-talk from what he'd called a *useless blob* would lead to such incredible adventures?

Thee end!
The end.

Thanks for being
my dance partner!

Love,
Konora

We'd jump for joy if we got a kind, honest review from a grown-up on Amazon, Barnes & Noble, or Goodreads.

We're a mom and daughter pair who were happily immersed in the ballet world until March of 2020. This project has been a labor of love, and it would mean the world to know it made someone happy.

THE DANCE-IT-OUT! COLLECTION

ONCE UPON A

Dance

SERIES CATALOG ALSO INCLUDES:

DANCING SHAPES · KONORA'S SHAPES · BALLET JOURNALS

www.ONCE UPON A DANCE.com

WATCH FOR SUBSCRIBER BONUS CONTENT

CPSIA information can be obtained
at www.ICGtesting.com
Printed in the USA
BVHW020611281022
649961BV00004B/64